Come Fly with Me

PAGE PUBLISHING, INC.
Conneaut Lake, PA

First originally published by Page Publishing 2021

ISBN 978-1-6624-2807-4 (hc)
ISBN 978-1-6624-2806-7 (digital)

Printed in the United States of America

Come Fly with Me

TOM LOCKIE

What a great evening. As I stroll across the ramp to my DC-7, I can smell the salt air and see the mountains off in the distance beyond the bay.

It's a perfect night for flying.

As I approach the plane, I see lots of people working on it. They look like a colony of ants crawling all over it. They're doing all sorts of things like loading the passenger bags and cargo we're carrying tonight. The mechanic is inspecting the plane, people are bringing food onboard, and the passengers are boarding. We'll be departing very soon.

"American Flight 2, you're cleared to New York's John F. Kennedy Airport via the Tahoe One Departure and the Denver Transition. Climb and maintain Flight Level two-three-zero. After departure, contact Bay Approach on frequency one-one-niner-point-five."

"Roger," we radio back to him.

That's pilot talk for, *Okay, we've got it.*

Now this particular airplane is *brand-new*. It's the pride of the fleet and the latest model of the DC-7. It has all the bells and whistles pilots like. My plane takes me to some pretty cool places, like New York City, on tonight's flight.

"American Flight 2, you're cleared to start engines and taxi."

As each engine comes to life, you can feel the vibration and smell the fuel and oil. The combination is a smell we pilots never forget. It always brings a smile to our faces because we know it's the smell of adventure. With all four propellers spinning, we can barely hear ourselves think. But we wouldn't have it any other way!

Now we're ready to taxi for takeoff.

Sitting on the runway, the other end seems so far away and about as wide as the sidewalk in front of my house! I can hold my thumb up and cover the other end of the runway—it's so far away! The flight to New York tonight is really long, almost eight hours! This means we need a lot of fuel to get us there, so our plane is *very* heavy, and we'll use the *entire runway for takeoff!*

"American Flight 2, you're cleared for takeoff," the tower calls.

We push the throttles up to takeoff power. Boy, you think it was noisy before? Now it's *so* loud as the four engines work to pull our big plane down the runway fast enough so we can fly. At the very end of the runway, the plane leaps off the ground and sails smoothly into the air. Our lumbering elephant on the ground turns into a graceful bird in the air.

"American Flight 2, turn right to a heading of zero-nine-zero and contact departure. Have a great flight."

"Have a great flight." I always love the sound of that! Our flight takes us over the San Francsico Bay. I can see the Golden Gate Bridge over my left shoulder as it slowly disappears into a fog bank that's moving toward the city.

Out in front of us, the Sierra Nevada Mountains are getting bigger and bigger in our front windows! It's like they're growing! Mountains can't grow! Well actually they can, but that's a different story! Anyway, *these* mountains are getting closer, and no matter how fast we climb, they seem to stay real close to us. When we level off at twenty-three *thousand* feet, they are just nine thousand feet below us. It feels like we can reach out and touch them. They seem so close!

The mountains and Lake Tahoe pass below us. Lake Tahoe is very cold and clear. It's really deep too! Mountains, rivers, and lakes give way to the desert, the Salt Flats, and the Rocky Mountains as our flight continues east toward New York City.

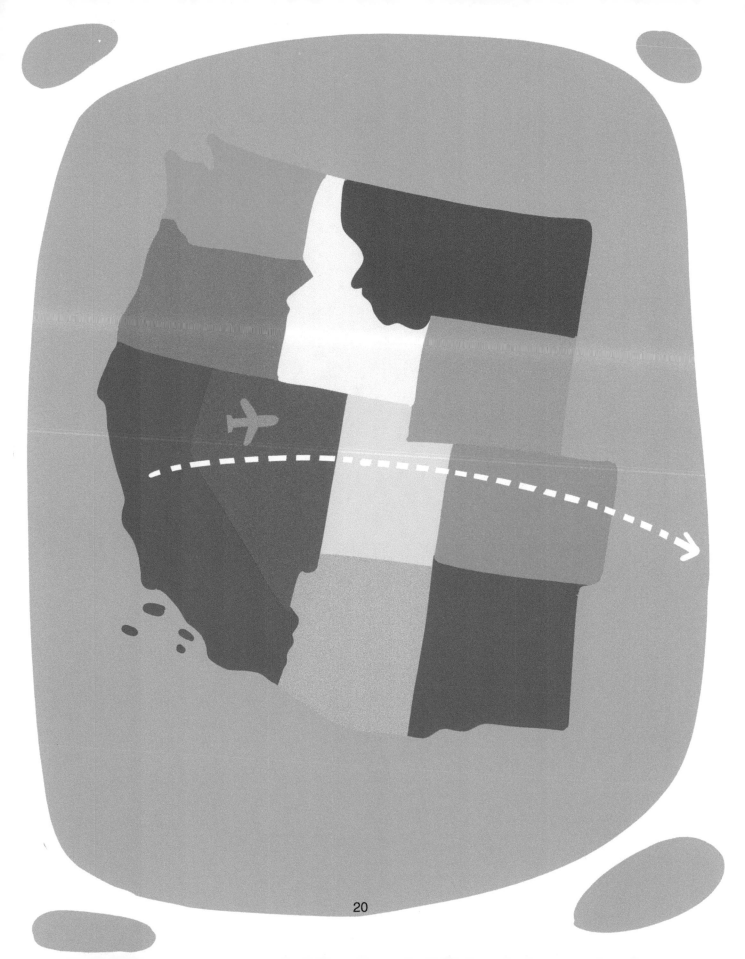

As the setting sun fades behlnd us to the west, night closes in. Everyone on the plane settles in for the eight-hour flight to New York. In the cockpit, we are all business. In the cabin, the passengers feel like they're in a restaurant that's moving over three hundred miles per hour! They even get pillows and blankets. It's a first-class ride for them.

There's no weather along our path, so we'll have a smooth ride. There's a full moon tonight too, so everything around us is lit up almost like daytime! City afer city go by, each lit by street lights and late night traffic. Everything seems so close. It seems like you can reach down, pick up the cars, and drive them like toy cars. It's like a dream.

As night gives way to morning, the sun slowly peeks above the horizon to look at us, and we stare right back. Morning is always a great time to fly, unless of course you've been flying all night! As the sun continues to light up the eastern sky, we can see the twinkling lights of New York City in the distance.

During our descent for landing, we fly close to the Statue of Liberty! What a great statue and what a great story she tells. For us, she marks the end of a long flight and entry into some of the busiest skies in America.

28

As we get close to the airport, we can see the runway lights. From up here, they look like the strings of lights you wrap around your Christmas tree. The runway looks so small, just like a sidewalk again!

Our DC-7 touches down smoothly, and I taxi her around the airport to our gate. It's a busy morning here at JFK with planes taxiing all over the place. It's like morning rush-hour traffic on the freeway!

The guideman stands at the gate and leads us to our parking spot. As the wheels roll to a stop, the copilot and I look at each other and smile.

"Another successful crossing," we say to each other.

That's the pilot talk for, *Whew, we made it!*

As I walk toward the terminal, I wonder what I like most about flying my DC-7. Is it the sights and sounds of the plane? Is it the excitement of takeoffs and landings? Could it be all the flying adventures? There are so many good things about flying I could never choose just one thing.

Maybe it's something simpler. My Dad was a pilot too, and he gave me a gift to enjoy until I could fly like him. Yep, I'm the Captain of my very own DC-7 model airplane! Like so many great adventures, this flight ended rather abruptly with, "Tommy, turn the lights back on in the living room and come to the kitchen. Dinner is ready!"

"Oh, Mom, do I have to?"

About the Author

Tom Lockie is an airline Captain with American Airlines. His father flew for American also. At an early age, Tom was given a gift by his Dad, the DC-7 mentioned in this story. His Dad gave him another gift too: the desire to fly. Tom's DC-7 saw many flights of fantasy and was well traveled before being retired for the real thing!